I0757400

GNASHING TEETH
PUBLISHING

_______ figuration: an anthology of trans writers

Table of Contents

Foreword

When I first sat down to write the foreword for this book, I wondered whether it was too *on the mark* to open with a Leslie Feinberg quote. Then as quickly as this thought arose, it imploded into ridiculousness. Trans writers, makers, creatives, thinkers, artists, and most importantly, people, have a target on their backs, not just in a broad historical or social justice context, but with precision and calculated hatred at this particular moment in time. While it might seem obvious to me to preface an anthology of emerging trans writers with words from our late, great, queer elder Leslie Feinberg, I realized that the point of this book is not to reinvent the wheel, but to exist within and honor the trans literary canon built for us since the advent of literature. Being trans isn't new, and being a queer writer trying to get your work out into the world isn't new, and systemic repression of the voices in this book isn't new, but I am introducing you to new voices anyway. As I am writing this, newly-reelected Trump threatens the safety and visibility of trans individuals within the United States, the recent UK Supreme Court ruling upholds that gender is based on biological sex, and colonial genocide projects in Palestine and beyond aim to eradicate generations of queer people. Now more than ever, it is time to repeat these words like a prayer, so here's the quote:

"Gender is the poetry each of us makes out of the language we are taught."
— Leslie Feinberg, *Trans Liberation: Beyond Pink or Blue*

Gender is poetry, but it is also fiction, personal essay, experimental forms, hybridity. The works in this book defy genre, decorum, and biological sex. Within these pages, gender is literature. More than forty selected contributors are bending the parameters of language to make room for each other. Some of the writers you will encounter here are seasoned awardees, and for some, it's their first publication. The content of this book was gathered in response to an open call not just for writing on trans topics, but writing about anything by trans writers. Chroniclers from the world over offered the brave gift of their words. In this way, I feel that the prefix *trans* meaning across is accurate. We are together offering a collection across generation, genre, demographic and experience to become a drop in the beautiful, wide lagoon of queer literature.

One of my dearest mentors is the poet and activist CA Conrad. A poem of theirs I refer to often is "Acclimating to the Comfort of the System Breaking Beneath Us," from the book *Amanda Paradise*. CA gave me this book the first time we shared a meal together, and I'd like to leave you with a line from the poem as you approach our collection with the grace and grit of our present moment:

> *are you sure we can handle this*
> > *because I am absolutely certain*

The writers and artists in this book will leave an indelible print on trans literature, but more importantly, on trans community, rage, and hope. *___figuration* does not necessarily refer to the identity transformation of the writers included here, but of the exaltation of their words. Let this work change you. In its generosity I am absolutely certain.

L Scully

Reaching
Sarena Brown

My Jesus is a Drag Queen
Cloud Sinclair

she struts and twirls on high heels

gives me a fiver from her push up bra and when i tell her there's a cost of living crisis she adds an extra few pence and a kiss on the cheek for good luck. i see her at church in the back row laughing absurdly at the fake supermarket jesus on display besides the pastor. she pops the wheels on cop cars and sings hymns with the homeless. she knocks on my door late at night, forehead against the wood asking for a place to spend the night and of course i oblige. i see her in the gay bar on tuesday night her show runs until the early hours "see the son of god work a pole!" the flyer reads. i meet her in the back alley. i smell of oranges and french coffee but all the saints in heaven have nothing on her. blessed be the jockstrap. blessed be us. beautiful humanity dancing in the heated palm of destruction.

the warm weather resides at baggage claim –
Zofia Provizer

i recited
ocean of tears
to remember what the other
word for carousel is - which is
baggage claim - i wish i had
a fatter ass - i went off
my meds and feel
the same - meaning -
i cry myself to sleep - sometimes - singing
hallelu you - hallelu me - to
the real housewives of new york city
on the muted screen -
the dryers do their job - revolve
in circles - it gives me
nausea - it gives me
connection - on any given day
- there is someone gorgeous here - too good
to wait - on the plastic child size chairs
- on any given day - i am
one of them - but today i have
my stank face on - when i take the day
off work - it is to come here - it is to
set a timer -
laundry - busses - oven - T.V. -
7th graders addicted to their screens -
they cannot unplug - i become
a bug - in their ears - you'll hear my voice until -
the chromebook closes - they say
sure faggot - take another
day off -

My Pretty Girl
Lucas Simone

I eat smuckers from the jar with my pretty girl as we decide how nude to get on this nudist beach. It turns out to be: feel how the sun feels in each layer of clothes. We both find our preferred coverage and switch it up when the clouds plump. We also light a fire, and we do it with matches too because lighters are gross and have gasoline in them like bad boats. We also walk to Skatepark Steven's tidepools and drop our spent matches in them and sometimes when we drop them and they're still on fire they make a little squeak like when you blow your nose after getting off the airplane. We also eat spaghettios from the can and we eat it with a seashell as a spoon because our fingernails and finger creases are totally smuckered. Sleeping on the beach won't work, my pretty girl says, because the sand is a billion years too young, which means: it's still fat rocks, and they're not smooth either. Skatepark Steven opens a soda and it sounds like a gunshot.

"You think they bring their own rocks when they make the railroad?"

"Yes I do."

We walk along it, her with stiff legs and a stomp on each hash, me with my feet pigeon feet on the rail, and the rail is the same color as the ocean because the ocean is the same color as the sky.

"Is the desert sand or is it dirt?"

"Sand but it's like dirt because there isn't any actual dirt."

"What about mud?"

"There's no *water*."

My pretty girl's hair is box dyed and really well, which means: it's white like an elf. We set up to nap on the tarred parts of the tracks. It smells like a playground. It smells like I'm in socks and filling up a water balloon, and I can nap anywhere and not get hurt. "What are these? Crab arms?"

"Mm. Cigarettes."

Abolish the family is a practice of resistance
MK Thekkumkattil

I mean, care work is a practice of abolition,
Theory: when blood pours from
Stab wound, when bullet lodges in
Femur, when infection blackens
Flesh, when she declares the only certainty
In life is death, when asked, Will you leave
Your homeland, she rephrases it:
Will I die on Palestinian soil, or will I die
Somewhere else? I will die in Palestine,
I will die in Palestine, there is no question
I will die in Palestine, so you see the blood
Pouring from her pale, sallow cheeks
Matted in her hair,
You see the blood dry down her tiny
Body and you decide you will never again
Call families of birth, blood family,
Because there is another kind of family borne
From blood, the blood of wounded children
With no surviving family, another kind of family
That makes these children kin,
Knotting nets far beyond Palestine, a practice
Of care far beyond the legal, biological, genetic, a
Motherhood from expanding
Sense of self beyond, self, beyond
Biological kin, that creates *blood kin*:
Kinship from resistance.

Voice Lessons
Maple Scoresby

I bite my tongue.

Words chewed into pulp
are easier to swallow.

Men do the talking, so
what am I if I speak?

I take another bite and
swallow my pride.

Apologies bleed out
of my lips,

just like a real girl.

Be me

Jack Lennon

>Be me

>Too scared to approach girls irl

>No friends

>Self-esteem practically non-existent as long as I've been alive

>Lonely.jpeg

>Start playing popular dating sim

>Craving human interaction

>Push past voice telling me I'm pathetic

>I deserve to feel love, even if it's just from cute vidya game girl

>newdepthsreached.mov

>At first feel like I can't connect

>Mfw even fictional women don't like me

>After a while I start to get to know them

>They ask me questions

>No girl has ever asked me a question before

>Someone is interested in me

>Feelsgood.jpeg

>Tell them the truth about my pathetic life

>They react like I'm the biggest Chad in the universe

>Think it's awesome that I sit in my room alone all day playing vidya

>Think it's rad that I have no friends

>Think I'm cute despite never seeing my face

>dreamscomingtrue.jpg

>My favourite girl is Ibuki

>A literal angel

>One night before I log off she tells me to take care of myself

>Takes care of myself

>Start integrating taking care of myself into my life

>Use her as a reason to better myself

>Ibuki would want me to eat something other than chicken nuggies every
night

>Ibuki would want me to shower

>Ibuki would want me to dress well

>Ibuki would want me to look after my health

>Start hitting the gym
>Girls are noticing me
>Solid 7 hits on me at the gym
>Completely uninterested
>Tell her I have a gf
>Ask Ibuki to be my gf that night
>She says yes
>Mfw I have a gf for the first time in my life
>Our relationship is perfect
>All she does is ask me about my day
>What games I'm playing
>Tells me I'm the best boyfriend she's ever had
>Does that mean she's been with other guys
>Jealous.jpeg
>Start getting intrusive thoughts about Ibuki and other guys
>Sigma males stealing my girl
>Can't sleep
>Constant nightmares about giga Chads cucking me
>Know logically that she is inside a computer game
>She can't cheat on me
>Butwhatifshedid.png
>Start treating Ibuki really cold
>She notices
>What's wrong anon?
>Don't you love me anymore?
>Can't even answer her
>She is not my pure sweet baby angel anymore
>Plagued with visions of her getting dicked down by other guys
>Tell her to leave me alone
>She says nothing
>Disappears from screen
>MfwIfuckedup.jpg
>Feels bad
>Try to get her back
>She's gone
>Other girls tell me she's left the game forever
>Didn't know this was even possible

>Contact game devs
>They think I'm trolling
>Blocked and reported
>Maybe it's a bug they don't know about yet
>Try sharing online
>Post deleted due to not following mod rules
>Shit.png
>Keep playing game every day hoping she comes back
>Ibuki never shows up
>Give up on ever finding her again
>Begin dating girls irl
>Realise how good I had it
>Real life girls expect you to ask them questions back
>Have to hear about their day
>Boring.jpg
>They aren't impressed when I tell them I have no friends
>Most aren't into mmorpgs
>Also most girls are non-virgins and have ex bfs
>Insecurity flaring up again
>It's their fault for being sluts
>Blow up at a girl I met on Tinder in the middle of a crowded Starbucks
>Leave in tears
>Feellikepureshitjustwantherback.mov
>Try to find Ibuki in the dating sim one last time
>She's not there
>Succumb to the knowledge that I'm doomed to be alone forever
>Just before I log off forever
>Ibuki appears
>Hopeinhumanityrestored.doc
>*Anon, you must fix your heart*
>*I cannot help you*
>*Goodbye*
>Disappears
>Fucking slut

BOLOGNA

Lindi Dedek

If we didn't fall for pasta our fingers would

The tortelloni on display the truck the piazza
we stood back to back lighting up the queue
passing change to the window

we imagined your fingers soaking pasta fresca in vegetable
your fingers and your wife
           my wife and I cooked ours tonight
why why
we didn't invite you over

They Have Made Worm's Meat of Me

Alice Musgrove

I die every time I fall asleep.

Heaviness of limbs as proof of a stroke. The un/familiar falling sensation, evidence that my soul has jumped ship, self-preserving rat.

Dreams of my body turning black and caving in on itself, like when you put your thumb through an overripe orange.

Tearing myself from the brink.

Arms. Can they raise both arms in front of them? Rapid thumb-to-finger-and-back-again-in-the-darkness-of-morning motor skill tests.

Do I still have a conscience? Can I still love, hate, fear? Fear. Under the covers I am pink and firm. The walls of my stomach stand strong against the push of my thumbs.

Thundering heart beats.

search: What does a heart attack feel like? Heart attack symptoms? The NHS 111 online triage depends on knowing your registered sex at birth, not your gender identity.

I lost my registered sex at birth/between the cracks in the living room floorboards/on the backseats of the number 5 bus.

Sex is what's in your pants.

I go commando. Is that the UK or US version of pants? Pants are a product of fast fashion, which is a product of capitalism, which is a product of colonialism, which is a product of Empire, which is a product of greed, which is a product of (god? human nature? eldritch horrors beyond comprehension?)

You're dying, what does a bit of misgendering matter?

A part of me dies every time though. I turn to ice on your tongue though. It matters, though.

search: Heart attack symptoms in afab nonbinary people. Heart attack symptoms in people born as women. Heart attack symptoms in women.

Nightmares of my body turning black and caving in on itself. Their thumbs in my stomach, peeling back layers of skin and pith and fat and gristle. Nails carving she/her into my was/were hips.

In 1000 years, they'll dig up my body, and an AI-generated rendering of David Attenborough will dispassionately announce the discovery of a 24-year-old-female to those watching the darkness-of-morning-tv-slot.

Heartland
Maeve Vitelllo

I am at this point used
To the responses I get
From city queers when they
Learn I am from the midwest.
Something snide and
In-between apology and
Congratulation for my escape.

It is hard to summon
So much defense for a
Stolen piece of land
That wants me dead anyways but
I still try
whenever another urban Fag
acts like this entire
Country hasn't tried
And failed
to bury me
My whole life or

Like their concrete streets
Are some protection
Against a bloodlust
That runs as deep
And digs as hard
As in America.

Queer Americana
Maeve Vitello

I keep meaning to ask
How long until we have
Traditions too?
Or, I guess,
How long until us
Queer folk have enough left
Over for symbolism after
Paying the bills?

I look melancholy at
A midwest suburb
And lament what gets left
Behind in transition.

Queer people always say
They're escaping the Midwest
But I don't think that.
They always say they
Don't want that kind of
Americana
But I don't think that.

A city might let you
Change your name but won't
Remember it just the
Same as when
You came
And all we want is
To be known.

We don't want it
The way they have it
There but a painted fence
And a garden we keep

Green and a house big
Enough for the whole
Damn polycule. Now
Ain't that something
To work for?

October 2010

Jude Singer

Allie's parents lived near Kenilworth Park, in a house with three stories, including a basement apartment, and it was beautiful, and she was beautiful. Her family rented out the basement to a couple of recent college graduates. If we were outside and heard the jangle of one of the young adult's keys in their door, we'd run, too shy to talk to people in their twenties. The upstairs house was painted all white on the inside, white ceilings, white floors, white walls and white tables. Allie's mother made us play outside.

Kenilworth felt wild to us in the way a city park can only feel wild to urban children: it was, in our minds, vast, impenetrable. We did not call it the park but "the forest".

In Kenilworth Park, on the east side of the park in the part furthest away from the central playground, there are two rocks that in my young eyes were five, ten feet apart. And tall, too, stretching to at least my chest. And if you scrunched yourself up on the rock, if you bent your knees and rocked your weight forward hard enough, and if you weren't afraid of splitting your head open on the hard earth below, you could jump the distance. I was afraid, but Allie leapt.

Oregon was built to burn and in the October of 2010, when Allie and I were twelve or thirteen years old, the fires encroached upon Portland for the first time in our lives. The winds were heavy and had blown the fire towards us. Power lines had been downed, school was canceled because we could not breathe. The sun was a perfect orange circle like an egg yolk, the sky dyed a salmon gray from the smoke. The city itself did not burn, but my mother asked me not to go outside anyway. I left her a note on the fridge with a magnet. In those days, her reins on me were loose, almost an afterthought. I met Allie at Kenilworth. She had an orange bandana tied around the lower half of her face, covering her nose and mouth, like an outlaw. Like someone sharp and dangerous and toothy. When I got close, she pulled down the bandana.

"My dad gave me this," she said, "because of the smoke."

"Oh," I said. "Should I be wearing one, too?" She shrugged, and pulled the bandana back up. It bothered me that I could not see her mouth, but I didn't tell her.

When it became clear that my mother was right and our lungs were burning, we walked home, to my home, a little further from Kenilworth than Allie's. And as we walked out of the park, as we emerged from the forest and into the city street, we heard a great cracking noise, like thunder or a gunshot. I had never heard a gun fired, but I thought to myself, that is a gunshot. I looked at Allie, to say let's go home right now, but she was already jogging in the direction the noise came from. I did not think twice about following her.

We rounded the corner and saw that a tall, thick pine tree, one that lived on the border of sidewalk and park, had cracked open, tipped over and fallen onto the street. It was tall enough that it blocked both lanes of traffic. And it had landed on a car. The roof of the car had caved in and the cab of the car had a man inside and when I saw the man I stopped moving, because I could see that his body had been squished by the tree in ways that a human body is not supposed to be squished. I could see his blood. I could see some parts of the inside of his body.

Allie was not looking at the man, she was looking at the tree, her mouth a little open.

"Why did it fall?" She said. "I don't understand why it fell."

Other cars had stopped and there were adults crowded around the car with the man whose body had been squished. A woman left her own car idling and ran to a house on the other side of the street. She started pounding on the door, yelling for whoever was home to call an ambulance.

"The wind probably blew it over." I said. I grabbed her hand, tugging at it. "This is weird. Let's go home."

"No." She looked at me, her eyes were wide. "I want to watch."

So we stayed and watched, hand in hand, stood close enough together that our shoulders touched. The neighbor in the house that the woman was banging at opened the door, angry, and then his mouth gaped into an 'O' of shock when he saw what happened. They both disappeared into the house. An ambulance and a fire truck arrived a few minutes later, one right after the other. We watched them use tools like giant pruning shears to cut the car open, ease the man out onto the street, but it didn't matter because the man was already dead. His body had been crushed by the metal of his car which had been crushed by the wood of the tree.

We stayed until a man who had been in another car noticed us watching and yelled at us to get out of there, and then we ran home. The smoke settled in our lungs and made them ache. As always, with everything we did, I felt it doubly, as if Allie and I were psychic twins, her pain became mine, phantom.

to the Last Wild Wolf in Ireland
Kes Maro

killed in county carlow in 1786

we named you first MacTire— son of the land &
because we assumed that the son must look like his mother
we called the land Wolf Land

once-dense forest played nursery to your shy mirage
the moss grew to cushion your feet & the wind sang your lullaby
hush, fallen branches & dry leaves quiet their whispers
for you
like training wheels for stalking your next meal

more than a thousand years before the last moment
the annals claim that blood rained from the sky
& that wolves were heard speaking like humans
did you try to warn us then of what was coming?

six pounds for every bitch & less for each kind after
cromwell's afterimage
leaves instructions for conquerors
carved & recarved
into the hills of every place that remembers its conquering

First. it says.
Name every sharp-toothed-meat-eater Predator. Then
kill every predator. There must be nothing
scarier than you. When small and soft creatures
become overabundant. Name them Prey.
Do not differentiate between the rabbit and the person.

There can be no more mothers. No trees
cut them down equally. Collect the bodies. You
need them. You need them so bad.
For ships and houses and things

you can sell and sell with. They cannot be allowed
to have trees or to have mothers.

Second. Salt all but specially designated soil.
These are the Special-Growing-Zones.
If the soil does not feed you
Conqueror
first
then do not let it feed anyone at all.
Prey must be hungry
to stay Prey.

Third. When they call you savage
cruel
ravager tell them
that they are even worse
for having resisted you. Take
their unmothered children
and teach them of a God who loves them
oh so much but who acts
exactly like you do.

Then. cromwell's afterimage says. It will not matter
when you die. It will not matter for hundreds
and hundreds of years.
When you have made a whole people prey
it will take them centuries to imagine
unconquering themselves.

when they find the Last Wild Wolf in Ireland
they find her because she is killing sheep.
hungry & impatient. imagine her
with entrails & wool still tangled in her teeth. her survival too bloody for
unforested land.
she is unrepentant. she is furious.
I WAS HUNGRY, she screams.
I WAS SO FUCKING HUNGRY.

I AM ALL ALONE OUT HERE NOW.
THERE ARE NO TREES, NO ELK, NO RABBITS. NO
INSTRUMENTS FOR THE WIND TO SING THROUGH. THERE'S
JUST YOU AND THE SHEEP
AND I ATE THE SHEEP. I ATE
THE SHEEP.
in her hunger the wolf becomes prey

and then
they kill her.

What's Wrong With Me
Shae Hicks

What's wrong with me, really?
Nothing.
Everything.

Are we talking surface level or deeper than that?
I've got a few rolls, one big unnecessary hole
But is it wrong, am I wrong if I don't mind my flaws too much?
When I'm excited, sometimes my voice stays flat
Being happy and homed are my only real goals
I look bald and babyish in every single hat
I'd rather eat out of a can than a bowl.

What's wrong with me, really?
I'd rather let the doctors decide
While I sit comfy on the long couch and confide
Trauma dump every fucked up thing that's happened in my life.
I'm a broke, bow-legged, big foreheaded kinky freak
Despite thousands of pushups, I still feel weak
I'm not growing enough, apparently.

What's wrong with me, really?
I care too much what others think.
I care so much my cheeks turn pink
From holding a mirror in front of me
So I can be everything you want to see.

What's wrong with me, really?
I'm living.

The Other Moon
Elise Jeanmaire

I was riding my bike home with a towel over my shoulder, still dripping wet from laps around a sprinkler. It was dark, and I was late. My parents were probably pacing the house, stiff as streetlights, wondering where I could be. And I wondered where they could be—*in their heads.* They spent most of their time tracing the violence of a useless war thousands of miles away, hoping my brother was somewhere safe. As the deaths climbed, so did their tells: my dad's hands would shake when he picked up his coffee, and my mom never left the house, afraid she would miss an important call. The type of call that would end the nightmare or make it worse.

I was the second-born child, almost two decades between my brother and me. I know him through a filmstrip of pictures that line our staircase, the late Christmas cards in which he misspelled my name, and my parents, now husks drooping through the house.

I stopped my bike in the middle of our cul-de-sac. I could feel the cold dampness of my bathing suit when I inhaled and exhaled; cold belly and stuck fabric. I remember feeling something odd—a presence. I scanned the lush lawns, the homes labeled with American flags, and the dark corridors between each property. Nothing. No shadows, no squirrels, no people. So I looked up into the sky and noticed our moon, like a bowl of milk. And next to it, another moon! A moon as big as ours! Two moons in the sky! Side-by-side, like eyes set on a star-freckled face.

I yelled out, "MOM! DAD!"

They spat out of our house like they were retched.

"Honey, what is it? Are you okay?" my mom yelled.

I didn't say a word and slowly pointed at the sky.

"Jesus Christ!" my mother said, the cross around her neck leaped with each syllable.

My father, a reserved man whose work required dress shirts and slacks, looked up at the sky and said, plain as day, "What the fuck?"

I laughed. I couldn't help it. I'd never heard that word from his mouth before.

"Do we call someone?" my mom asked.

"Who do we call?" my father asked.

"I don't know. Do we call the cops?"

"It looks like eyeballs!" said my father. "Two big eyes, taking us in."

"Doesn't it!" I smiled at him, and he smiled back. It was the first time I'd seen them like this. Humans! Swearing humans! I loved them, and I wanted them to stay that way forever.

"No, no, just moons," my mother held to reality, afraid of where we would go if she didn't.

"What if it's an alien invasion?" my dad asked. Did my dad believe in aliens? I wanted my father-daughter dance right then! I wanted to ask him what else he believed in at his most vulnerable!

My mother wrapped her arms around me, protecting me from something she couldn't explain, but admiring the spectacle. It felt like fireworks on the fourth of July, the two of us, our faces glowing under the night's sky, dressed in wonder.

"It's truly something else," said my father.

We stood out there, together, as the night suckled at our souls.

The next day, the other moon was gone. People from all around said they'd seen it, but nobody had an explanation. The following day, we received the call. My mother's body hunched, as if all her bones had disappeared. My father's hands shook so hard his wedding ring beat against the kitchen table—*ting, ting, ting.*

The following night, my parents stood in the cul-de-sac and stared at the sky, wondering if the other moon would show up and give back what it had taken that night.

And I watched them from the window, waiting for them to return.

Two Excerpts
Jackie Barnes

im inspired by my friends ability to love themselves to let themselves have
needs and wants and comfort im so grateful they share this with me
while im maintaining my mental illnesses and exhibiting behaviours
im lucky to have such amazing friends
i wish i felt this way all the time
i wish i remembered to be more grateful for my life

i get cynical
when i feel this love

   i remember fear more than anything

   i am my own child

over and
      over and
 over and
over and
     over
       again

        do you remember how you felt about things as a kid

i have had help in the raising
but i raised myself
with anime
and books
and time spent away from home
being away from home was survival
the freedom and comradery
that was never going to exist at home
home was a hunting ground
small blocked spaces
only misunderstanding
and confusion
unclarity

home made the world worse
home shown the world in dark scary caverns   guaranteeing mistrust

i am my own loving father and mother **i am the love my father
imagined he gave to me** i am the care my mother forgot to show me i am
the protective arms my father thought he had **i am the attentiveness my
mother didn't give me** over and

        over and
over and
      over and over
     over and
  over and
   and
over and
  over

And we can smash it with sledgehammers.
Sarah Mike

In the back of my science class Galen made me terrified of cabinets. They lined the entire room, only the faux-marble counter halting their growth. Anything could be in those cabinets, he said. You could be. Then again, maybe I was the cabinet, forcing things no guest should ever see deep behind pantried goods and fresh folded linen. I was terrified of being a cabinet. I saw them everywhere, in the back of Galen's head, in the pit of my brother's stomach. Everything unsaid swept away.

A great deal of wood goes into building a cabinet. An absurd amount, really, if we were to divine the ultimate fate of one in the back of a home kitchen. Would it not be better for the environment to leave out things floating for all to see? To lay bare all we wish to lock away, to be honest about what expired food stalks the back row, to catch the green mold of bread before it jumps to the next loaf?

My whole life was a cabinet. My father, the treasurer, my brother in charge of Homeland Security, one of my friends was promoted to Secretary of Transportation when he got his first car, my Opa for Veterans Affairs. Of course I stuffed my cabinet with those I was closest. But I was no president, and though they advised me as best as they could, it was clear I was never fit for the job.

I want a daughter.

I want to watch her grow into a beautiful woman (she'll still have freckles, and curly hair, but it will be dyed a deep, tuna red), then invent time travel, and go back decades, crawl through that cabinet in science class, and offer to take my place, and she will live out my life the way it should have been lived, redo it all without error.

And then I can go to Fiji, and I can live on the lapis waves, fishing for my meals, and I'll only have one change of clothes, and I won't store anything in cabinets, and then my future daughter can check on me, I can see how much better my life has been as her, and I can thank her, and maybe at the end she'll bring me a chipped and tarnished cabinet, and we can smash it with sledgehammers.

Popcorn Lung
Calvin Jones

As the cottonwood sperm snowed all around, we sat on the bench
with two of your dispos & I pretended they were working,
in the car after you asked me so are you high? Yeah I think a
little, except mostly my lungs just scraped as I talked. Your
girlfriend doesn't like drugs, or your boyfriend I mean, & you
are the girlfriend, maybe. We 3 are never quite sure what to call
each other: such is the beauty of the closeted tranny. The lies
to parents, the pronoun slips, the lies to each other, we're fucking
garbage queers. I leave to sit in my car outside so you and he
have time alone, it is night, I scare easily, do crosswords.
Maybe my gender is third wheeler. Maybe it's when I really do
get high & you keep telling me to shut the fuck up. Maybe it's
your I-love-yous. No pill for that. You're barreling into addiction,
we're plummeting towards partition, highway-driving through
the blizzard, binging carts & Hobo Johnson, hydroplaning, sucking
on the plastic, burning the midnight oil, you bought acid & we're
swallowing eggshells.

field notes
Max Gregg

field notes: grace church, red hill

kudzu grows over the exterior façade. anik's lidar scanner takes an impression of the interior. they map the sanctuary with their phone camera. across the screen, the grid, 3D and neon green is spidering.

 it blazes over rafters, pews, the high wooden beams, the cross someone has stuck the number 69 on, where parishioners once knelt. it obliterates the time i tried to fuck here, exposed yellow insulation where the ceiling's opened out.

then, behind the mirror the anti-kitchen bulges,
a tumor or the lining of a cave.

field notes: grace church, red hill

there are two churches. the new one's down the road now, and up the higher hill. when the congregation moved locations, they moved like a people raptured. they left it all behind. censors, the vestments, the episcopal bible with its red font.

anik has since torn out the pews, peeled off the vinyl and hung it up in sheets of flayed synthetic skin. what's underneath is some kind of toxic soft foam, a skeleton of wood to be repurposed. the bitten inside of the cheek is, it may be that in writing this, i'm going deeper inside a mirror i've mistaken for a cave. reenacting the protestant reformation as a striptease.

grace notes

i am over there, here where I am not
like a sword the night glints off of in the desert
ideation sometimes takes on density
a neon green spidering over rafters,
pews, the lofty beams, echoes of
future iterations

you see the sun glow out the gaping hole
what is church without confession
a skeleton of wood
this mirror exists, as does the tongue
i've decided to be grateful

Gas Leak
Tommy V.W.

Blue-lipped on a milk crate,
Chef resurrects me
with lemon medallions

and ice. I praise God
for lack of heat,

lack of poisonous gas:
an invisible heavy

on the line. I am small,
a canary,

if you will. A foreign spot:
colder and sicker

than the other guys.
Invisibly lacking,

I stick around. I cut
chicken in the back,

breasts cool and glistening
like exposed organs in my hands.

October In Luleå
Iona Carmine Roisin

In Northern Sweden I see two swans migrating. I'm disappointed about my future. Projecting onto the other fat person at the breakfast buffet. They go for seconds, then thirds. It's obscene that I notice. Stifle a cough because why not. Got tense from folding inwards, shallow breathing, chewing politely. Shrinking as much as possible while still bound to form, a beer can underfoot. The fish gets worse as I chew it. I'm full of regrets. Though enough of this place to eat a pickle at breakfast, yes before noon even. Mostly I eat a lot of white bread, my friend Anna says it's of the devil. My gut agrees but it's sensitive to everything, like dairy or waiting for someone I shouldn't love to text me.   The rain hits like I'm a child and every low hanging cloud enters my fist heart. Tramping about in wet boots, I search for an as-yet-undisclosed revelation. All I find is dull feeling, tourist office. The autumn purple of newly stripped branches pierces me. I'm not ready. No one asks, but I still imagine telling people that I am here trying to cultivate my reverence. Instead of the actual reason which is: no reason.   Luckily I sleep well in an expensive bed. I try to channel some ancestors to press my woes upon but they're all elsewhere, no urgency in them. Probably rehashing family tragedies, like the one who burned *god rest his soul*, like the one who was exiled, spitting over ghost shoulders at the mere mention. I can't say how I came to be here but what you forget is just as holy as what you remember, probably, and I know that most of a person's life is lived in the place between these bookends. Full yet unspecific.   On the bus I touch a maroon leather seat, it touches back, remembers how it used to be warmed from the inside, alive even. It's surprisingly easy to permit yourself to be hurt, to be turned into a semi-functional object for another's convenience. I watch the moon strobe on an unknown body of water as I leave. The road moves forward so the reflection does too, shivers, alive even. I think: that's the most beautiful thing I've ever seen.

I want to love my brother
Judah Coffman

I want to love my brother
But I don't know how
and I never knew I was allowed.

I always assumed that at some point,
I missed a lesson in school
when the teacher pulled the students close
and told them, "You can't tell anyone I told you this,
but you *can* do what you want to do.
It's not just for the people who were born happy."

I wonder if some things are so precious, so true
that no one dares say them out loud
as though making them real
makes them, at the same time, ripe for the taking
Until they can never exist again.

Is bad always big?
Can good only be small?
Can my God match them in size?

Your butt is so nice
f.f. kahani

I watch you

press up against the lid of my breath

a gleam catching as my
pocket lips swallow your optic nerve,
I skim your skin and enter the dark
dome: my pilgrimage to this unknown where you swell and
                      s p r e a d
                      I wedge into you

heavy drops river
   d

      o

      w

      n

your back – chasm
as I pull   jewel   after   jewel

is it okay to make a *mes*_{*s*}
to make a love

The Rave
Jo Weinberg

everyone thinks
they're autistic
she's flipping
me off as
a joke
everyone thinks
they're a genius
paranoid on
cold tiled floor
somewhere between
cream and sugar
explosive diarrhea
the music is shit
everyone thinks
I'm annoying
she's bullying me
as a joke
she's wiping down
the countertop with
peony blossom
soap
everyone thinks
we're together
ponytail pendulums
whips my cheek
the *yeah*
in the sky
the *yeah*
in your mouth
everyone thinks they're a DJ
I'm a real tough guy
everyone thinks I'm a girl
pouting competition
it's a tie

let you win though
everyone smokes
out my window
she kisses me
as a joke

Trans Manifesto
Robin Arble

for Blue
before and after
Eileen Myles

on our way to
NYC

pushing 90
in the pass lane

our bodies move
before we do

pulling
over and

shitting in the
men's restroom

of a McDonald's in
Connecticut

shouldn't we
have a third stall

just for us
clocky girls

too femme for
urinals but can't

fake that hissing
sitting down?

Nothing more
trans than

almost clogging
the wrong toilet

The Waiting List on a Sinking Ship
Kate Hunneyball

The queue stretched to the back of the ship and into the rising water. It inched through the chaos towards the lifeboats at the front, where sailors grunted and strained at the winches. The screams from down below grew louder, so the band played soothing holding music over them. Officers were shouting "Women and children first!", presumably because children are our future and women are required to make more children.

By the time I reached the front, my ankles were wet. I met a very official-looking officer there, who was acting as the evacuation conductor.

"Miss H-? Yes," the conductor nodded. His eyes were inscrutable under the shadow of his cap. "You're definitely on the list."

"Great," I replied. "And how long is the list? Because there's quite a lot of water…"

I shivered in my dress, hoping that, if I looked desperate and wretched enough, they'd bump me up the list. Not too wretched though, or they may mistake me for a third-class passenger. But the conductor simply glanced at my bare shoulders and sniffed.

"It won't be long."

I nodded to confirm my comprehension – not because I particularly felt like nodding – and stepped aside to let other passengers through. The next one seemed to transition seamlessly from the queue to the lifeboats. As did the next. I watched passenger after passenger board the small boats before me, and I couldn't help wondering what they had that I didn't.

Perhaps they had all secured a place on the waiting list *before* the ship started sinking. That would at least be fair. But then, what kind of ship makes you *opt-in* for a lifeboat? That's hardly the first thing on one's mind when boarding a cruise. It ranks, naturally, far behind the first-class bar and falls even further behind after a couple of mint juleps. This was hardly the kind of service one expects on the "World's Greatest Steamer".

"Pardon me," I approached the Conductor again. "Will it be much longer?"

"We cannot share information regarding the list, ma'am. Please wait your turn."

"Yes, but I really must protest. I've seen several people board ahead of me. The water will be at my knees soon, why must I wait? I'd benefit from not drowning as much as the next."

"We're letting women and children on first."

"Oh, you should have said so sooner! I am a woman," I said, smiling womanly. "So this has all been one big misunderstanding…"

He looked me up and down like he possessed an X-ray machine in his head.

"You are?"

"Yes, indeed."

"I'm not empowered to say. All I know is, you're on the list."

Rejected, I retreated to the edge of the deck, hoping that a sea view would soothe my stinging pride. But it was considerably angled since the last time I'd seen it. And the sea was all darkness, except for an enormous iceberg glaring at us from a mile or so off. Below me, the water churned with flailing arms and falling bodies. You'd have to be inhuman not to be rent apart by their desperate cries, so I tore my handkerchief into strips and shoved them into my ears.

Class was undeniably a factor in the list. If I was first-class, I'd have been escorted safely to a warm, comfortable boat. However, if I was third, I'd have already drowned in the lower levels. At least they were lost together though. Yes, it was sick to leave hundreds to drown simply due to the position of their birth, but it was another kind of cruel to single one out to die alone, all for the sake of a list.

Suddenly, someone rushed past me, almost knocking me overboard. I whirled around and witnessed a kerfuffle of the highest drama.

"Excuse me," I protested to the conductor. "I just watched Kate Winslet and Leonardo DiCaprio board that lifeboat, and the only list they're on is in *Forbes*."

"There aren't any errors with the list."

"But Leo's a man! He might look like a lesbian, but-"

"You *may* be a woman, ma'am." He furrowed his brow. "But, I've been reliably informed, not the kind of woman included in our policy."

"Well, what is the right kind of woman?" I stammered. "At least let me try."

"Women who can have children. Like Kate Winslet."

I sighed. I couldn't try to be that. She was People Magazine's 49th hottest woman in 2005. I was barely a person.

Away from the lifeboats, I considered my options. There weren't many. The ship had nearly reached a 45-degree angle and time was thin.

I could always keep waiting. There was a chance that, once all the right people had been boarded and seated, the list would finally remember me. But what would that mean? To participate in a broken system and survive on luck and indifference. That was no justice. And I'd rather die than give the conductor the satisfaction of seeing me in his boat.

No, the list was over for me. I cast my eyes over the deck. There had to be another way to survive. There was always another way. I could fasten the wooden furniture into a raft, but they were now sliding down the deck into oblivion. Barrells float, but they'd be down in the kitchens, under the water. Perhaps if I'd quit the list sooner I could have emptied one and rode it to freedom. But, alas, I thought I could trust conductors. I was second-class, after all.

Violence was technically an option. Perhaps I could fight my way onto a lifeboat? If I wasn't the right kind of woman, I must be more than a match for the conductor.

My mind was racing, but my body was freezing and tired. So tired. Any daring plans I could conjure were beyond me now. Waiting had taken the fight out of me.

I could jump. Go the way of the wooden furniture and the third-class passengers. Join the churning, black waves. That'd show them. All it took was a single step off the edge and I'd be in the depths of oblivion. Perhaps one day someone would find my bones at the bottom of the ocean. They'd pry open my skeletal fingers to find my dignity intact. And they'd mourn for me, knowing what I'd sacrificed to keep it…

I was so surrounded by morbid thoughts, that I hadn't noticed the deck was almost empty. The crowd had all disembarked and only a handful of stragglers remained. But still, the conductors stood guard around the remaining boats.

The stragglers were a queer sight: oddly shaped, dressed strangely in gaudy gowns or gloomy suits, and of all different sizes. It was as if a great machine had sucked up all the men, women and children, leaving only the dregs at the bottom. While staring at them in the dim starlight, I 43dminist that I was left behind too. They weren't the right kind of person either. They were not Leonardo Dicaprio or Kate Winslet, like me.

For a moment, it occurred to me that we were many and the conductors were few. We could seize their pistols and commandeer a boat for ourselves. Perhaps even sail off to a new world, free from waiting lists and icebergs. But then a mighty groan erupted from the bowels of the ship, and it was all too late.

The ship had reached almost 90 degrees. The officers tumbled down the length of the deck like little toy soldiers. The head conductor cracked his head on one of his own lifeboats, dashing his brains across its hull. I watched them both fall into the jaws of judgement.

The non-Leos and Kates and I were left alone at last. No one spoke. What was there to say? My mind went to the first place it always did: the bar. There'd be no line for drinks, and waiting was thirsty work. I grabbed the nearest Anti-Leo by the hand and led the rest to the first-class lounge. It would be easier to plan our new life under the sea with a mint julep in hand.

Untitled
Kid Heathen

tender whatever,
Maya Cordero

I hide my pussy in your pussy,
I feed you collard greens.
I take this opportunity to tell you
that I wish you'd put a baby inside me.
I name them something gender neutral.
I raise them till they're dead.
I kiss your feet, I suck your toes,
I think Damn, I wish I knew
some quotes from the Bible.
Holy whatever, drunk and silly,
I hide my pussy in your pussy,
I build an altar in your name,
tender whatever, soft skinned hooligan,

(I Am) A Self-Replicating Disaster Made Of Weddings In My Body
Cassandra Whitaker

There is something to be celebrated there is
something to be celebrated there is something to be
celebrated —the name ringing out —in the echo
of the hallway —in the echo of celebration there
is a name —only one —only one —new name
It is celebrated It is celebrated It is celebrated It is
celebrated The first wedding I saw I was a small child
in a small Church in a small town in a small county
barely big enough to shout When my mother told me
that I would grow up to be a boy —I would grow up
to be a man —I didn't believe it —I didn't
believe that I would grow up The wedding that used to
reside in my wrists —a red wedding in the left arm
—a carefully chosen spot With my right hand I could
scratch a name —with my right hand I could scratch
an exclamation point—skin threatening to expand
under the cut What did I want to find there? What
did I want to return to? Every moment I touched it
—the wound—all those years ago —day after day
after day repeating the same gesture Now there is a
clapping Now there is a symbol dashing —a wedding
in my toe —in my finger bone —in the first rib
in the last rib —each wedding celebrating —a name

This Bill

Joel Sedano

This Bill

represent   s   so me

all   re

sent   u   sh all   re pent   re

presents   all

resent s   u

all   shall   se

pent   WHO   re

present   s   u

shall   all

re   sent

me   so me   sh all   re

pent

u all   re   present   me

re   pent

Driver

sterling-elizabeth arcadia

as a way of proposing a solution for my asexuality my roommate asks me if I can just tell my dates I don't want sex and I reply that no, I can't, and explain that while I don't want *sex*, per se, I do want *sex*, if that makes sense? Driving the pine barrens scenic byway I think of L, of B. the only birds I see the whole drive are turkey vultures.

Television at 14
Cecilia Inessa

Shotgun blast down the stairs
ruins her leather jacket

She lives but I'm transfixed: I want her coat, her bangs
and buckshot sprayed furious into my
quivering chest.

Jacq hymn
Jacq Roderick
After Wanda Coleman

Jacq. Just 'cause you're broke doesn't mean
jack. It takes one to be one. A
jack is a friend enclosed in a flush. A
jack that follows a king and queen is just that. A
jack. Speaking of they're never women, just
jacks. The beauty in being a fool isn't worth
jackshit. When you forget to be playful you
jack it. The ruse
jack thin slippery weasel-slick
Jacq. It takes one to be one. A
jacq is a thief & a friend.

Final Exam

Emma Schorin

This is an exam that measures you.

Name: ________________________________

Deadname: ____________________________

Date: ________________________________

I.   <u>Personality Test.</u>

Mark the answer that best describes yourself.

1. You've always liked tests, but you're worried…

a) …that's classist.
b) …that's alienating.
c) …that's unsympathetic.
d) …you're wrong.

2. Actually, you've always liked school, but you know…

a) …it's not for everyone.
b) …that's a you problem.
c) …you'll never go back.
d) …you have poor self-esteem.

3. You like books that…

a) …are valuable.
b) …are formally interesting.
c) …make you seem formally interesting.
d) …are short.

4.   You like men that…

a)   …are valuable.
b)   …are formally interesting.
c)   …make you seem formally interesting.
d)   …are tall.

5.   You like non-men, too, because they…

a)   …compliment your hair.
b)   …are funny.
c)   …smell good.
d)   …have taste.

6.   More than anything, you want…

a) …a time machine.

b) …children.

c) …rest.

d) …touch.

7.   Your favorite topic of conversation is.…

a) …boys.

b) …pseudoscience.

c) …the 1994 surprise hit *Muriel's Wedding*.

d) …yourself.

8.   A perfect Saturday night looks like…

a) …procrasti-baking, kissing, and a good book.

b) …chemical castration, baths, and other forms of palliative care.

c) …marijuana, pizza, and pizza.

d) …two friends, a bottle of wine, and the 1994 surprise hit *Muriel's Wedding*.

9. A literal Sunday morning looks like…

a)   …the comedown.
b)   …the comedown.
c)   …the comedown.
d)   …all of the above.

10. You are…

a)   …not funny.
b)   …not smart.
c)   …not kind.
d)   …scared.

II.   <u>Logic & Reasoning.</u>

Mark the answer that is most honest.

1.   Do you remember why you included this section?

a)   No.
b)   A little…
c)   Maybe.
d)   You'll never take me alive.

2.   If most people in school are better, and have always been better, at logic & reasoning than you, what statement is likely true?

a)   I am an illogical and unreasonable person.
b)   I am less logical and less reasonable than the average person.
c)   I am not an average person.
d)   I am not a person.

3.   A scared little girl inside a scared little boy eats too much. She eats as if there is no body to feed. If that's the only problem, how can you stop the child from eating?

a)   Remove the girl.
b)   Remove the boy.
c)   Remove the body.
d)   Remove the food.

4.   What did *you* do?

a)   I still don't know.
b)   I still don't know.
c)   I still don't know.
d)   I had other problems.

5.   If joking is a form of lying, then what is a class clown?

a)   A liar.
b)   A joker.
c)   A joke.
d)   Nothing, thank god.

6.   If a writer is a liar, and liars don't know how to stop lying, who will ever love you?

a)   Another liar.
b)   Another writer.
c)   Yourself.
d)   My mother.

III.   <u>Complete the Sentence.</u>

Mark the answer that fits the intended meaning.

1.   There is no easy way to say ___________________.

a)   I love you
b)   you love yourself
c)   goodbye
d)   Worcestershire

2. What is impossible for the ________________ is possible for the ______________.

a) fat kid   funny kid
b) trans girl   Bono
c) writer   lover
d) soy latte   bio-identical estrogen

3. Where there's a _____________________ there's a ________________.

a) will   lawyer
b) premise   story
c) worm   wormhole
d) human sacrifice   human being

4. Too many ________________ will spoil the ________________.

a) cooks   appetite
b) parents   self-esteem
c) prayers   faith
d) anti-depressants   libido

5. Loving ________________ requires loving ________________.

a) food   moderation
b) others   your work
c) art   taste
d) yourself   yourself

6. If you want _____________________, you have to sacrifice
    _____________________ for _____________________.

    a) anything   time   success
    b) happiness   your standards   a movie kiss
    c) to win   safety   victory
    d) me   your mind   mine

7. To you, writing is just _________________ without knowing
    _________________ or even _________________.

    a) a pilgrimage   where you're going   whose heart you're
                                              cating
    b) a potluck   who else was invited who's hosting
    c) a joke   what's funny   a punchline
    d) the only thing what else is out there why you'd look

8. You are _________________, not _________________, unless you
    _________________.

    a) alive   dead   kill yourself
    b) a girl   a boy   run out of pills
    c) happy   unhappy   run out of pills
    d) a writer   a joke   stop writing

9. Don't

    ____

    _________________.

    a) forget
    b) remember
    c) remember
    d) remember

IV.   <u>Reading Comprehension.</u>

Once upon a time, there was a little boy who loved princesses. He wore dresses sometimes but mostly because his friends did; he actually preferred being with the girls who didn't wear dresses, the girls who are now all lesbians with middle-parted hair and pronouns. His favorite princesses were Aurora, who slept, and Ariel, who traded her ability to speak for feet.

That's the uninteresting part of the story, though, so don't worry if you're not interested. The interesting part of the story, if you can call it that, is that the boy wanted a pet. Jasmine had a tiger; Belle had the Beast. Surely, he deserved something as compensation for not being able to exist yet? But the boy's parents said, no. They wouldn't let him have even a goldfish.

"You're irresponsible," they said. "You don't know what you want," they said when he asked again. "Life is a responsibility," they said a third time. The boy was puzzled but serene. The boy was often serene except when he was freakishly angry and didn't know why. But the boy was serene this time because he trusted his parents. He trusted that they knew best and he didn't.

Once, the boy took a walk alone in the woods. There were woods behind their house in the summer where the boy could be away from the other boys. The boy liked the shade, the wet air, the cool moss strapped to the sides of trees like band-aids. The boy liked the cool moss so much he collected it in his pocket, unaware that to do so was murder.

On this walk through the woods, the boy crossed a stream that had not been there the day before. And yet, it hadn't rained the day before. And yet, the stream was there. We know this because the boy crossed it. Interestingly, the other side of the stream was completely dry. There was nothing wet there, no moss, no air. The trees that grew there were spindly and frightening. The sound of the stream was silent from this side, and walking alongside its silent flow, the boy spied a frog buried in leaves.

The frog was as big as the boy's tiny fist. Its eyes were blueberries that watched the boy move closer and closer until the boy was eye to eye with the frog. He went flat on his chest so that he could see the frog; the leaves were dry here, so nobody would know that the boy was lying on the forest floor with frogs. The boy stared at the frog and the frog at the boy. The boy thought that the frog could be his pet, that he could take the frog home. A frog would make a marvelous pet; toads were *Harry Potter*-compatible, and frogs were like toads.

Then the boy had another thought. Perhaps this frog was not a frog at all. There was so much magic in the woods in those days. A white-haired woman sold chicken feet without the chicken. Wild dogs snapped themselves off of dead logs and howled. And the stream was dry on this side. Minor magic, but magic nonetheless, the boy thought. Perhaps the magic of the stream meant there was magic, here, with this frog, who may in fact be a prince. In that moment, the boy realized he didn't want a pet. He wanted a prince.

The frog had wide, flat lips. The lips looked like they'd been iced onto a frog-shaped cake, and the boy noticed, as he got closer with his own lips, that the frog kept licking its mouth with its bubblegum-pink tongue. This felt like consent. The boy had only ever kissed his best friend, who later said she didn't like it. He agreed. Kissing was strange, and disorientating. When he kissed his best friend, he felt like he wasn't in his body – in a bad way.

Just as the boy was about to kiss the frog, it leapt forward! The boy was so startled that he opened his mouth – wide enough for the frog to jump down the boy's throat. The boy coughed. The boy shuddered. The boy cried. The boy cried and coughed and cried but the frog would not come out. The boy could breathe, the boy could choke, the boy could swallow. But the frog would not come out. Not knowing what else to do, the boy goes home. He does not tell his parents where he was. He does not cross streams. He does not know why, but he has the terrible feeling that he has squandered a chance that he will never have again.

1. What meaning is the story intended to reflect?

a) Boys should be better supervised.
b) We must protect our nation's dwindling reserves of magic.
c) Amphibians are untrustworthy because of their dual nature.
d) Progress isn't linear, exponential, or even necessary.

2. Who do you feel bad for in the story and why?

a) The boy because he wanted something he couldn't have.
b) The frog because he probably died.
c) The boy's parents because they have a confusing child.
d) Yourself, the reader, for having to read it.

3. How is this story supposed to make you feel?

a) Sticky.
b) Guilty.
c) Confused.
d) Grateful.

4. How are stories supposed to make you feel?

a) Beautiful.
b) Sad.
c) Smart.
d) Like the 1994 surprise hit *Muriel's Wedding*.

5.   How do you feel now?

a) Sick.
b) Tired.
c) Sick and tired.
d) Like there's still a frog in your throat.

V.   <u>Essay.</u>

*Please respond in 100 words or fewer.**

Why can't it be you?

____

____

____

____

____

____

____

**If you need more space, write on your lover's hand..*

the end of something
Nomi Burjorjee van Pelt

in my throat there is a stack of stones
round smooth porous
they click together when I swallow
clatter when I speak

in the cards there is a heart suspended
between three swords
branch with new growth
lion, tail between legs
space for me to balance on my head

in her portrait she is wasted and cruel
I I tell
the 61dminis hotel seemed like a cool place to be
if you were hungry and fatherless

Public Restroom
Frances Coombe

PLASTIC FLOWERS IN FRESH
WATER
A LINE OF PEOPLE HOLDING
THEIR URINE

PLASTIC FLOWERS IN FRESH
WATER

Throwaway
MJ Griego

The news said we had a rat problem
I think the problem is the trash-bin bodies in the streets
and the rats are cute things
Dirty and smart to survive like this

I am rustling through the fools' silver plastic of a meal replacement bar
and cry over you on the cliffs' edge at the park
glass shards on the asphalt below, wet like it was me they dripped out of.
People are nothing but their bald spots to me like this,
spaces where things don't grow anymore

I am trying to make my way home
thinking about endings:
the funeral of my food wrapper
false promise turned garbage
passing sickly grasses cut

There's something contorted red and dead I avoid on the sidewalk
a body I can't name
I wonder how many of us will turn away.
I wonder how many of us will only look
before someone is brave enough to
discard it

in the only version of events
Clio Lake

1.

      in the only version of events i see proceeding all our desperate fucking bleeds into the last our regularity spins attracts mass becomes hot volcanic and micro-organism-bearing, stopping E makes me sick and feral and unwieldy and swelter in your dad arms when we fuck my come is sticky pungeant globular not dewey sweet and see-through rosehip syrup, our smell together altogether key-lime sours, you piss on tests my hair takes oil branches of fat retreat from my tits until your chest swells your nipples darken circled by wisps i feed on your neck our breathy 'i love you's' become incantations 'my body is an interdimensional portal' you say mouth full i repeat lapping at your pulsing clit my arms and legs grow thorns and bristles and my tongue barbs.

2.

      what kind of ———— am i to you bodiless or bathed in —— what righteous urge you have what enemy you think of me and them with me and how you fear our possibility

      how does it feel to be stagnant when we are inevitable when you keep —— us and we stay inevitable i kept my —— to use it to —— you with let that affront you or gag you or rattle your pearls

      i can tell that none of you're straight ———— you look you can't stop — (un)fuckable / unintelligible do you / stay away from our children / do you want to share anything with anyone about your desire

      creep / chaser / predator / grin
      to be housed in a women's prison; that's what the sex change's for / when the time comes to be housed in a women's prison / administrative task eugenics task what kind of — what —— adjudication of ——

      fear our offspring our little gods to eat your heads

The world has been this way for a long time.
Vincent Endwell

The world has been this way for a long time.

I was thinking, after I dropped your daughter off at the fields, how many years we have all been living just at the precipice, waiting for the drop. Beneath the floating city, the soccer fields still sit beside the storage units and paths climb up to the water towers, hidden in the trees. I remember as a teen coming here, loitering up by the towers. We would sit on the concrete and have conversations too deep for three in the afternoon. Now your daughter is reaching the age when those little dirt paths in the woods will belong to her.

It is funny the things that are passed on, the world order that remains. We live in a lineage whether we want to or not, one built on the ruins of every time past. The city cast a shadow over the valley as I headed out to Trisha's, its hot wind buffeting the car like a leaf, and in many regards I consider the builders' efforts a way of building without ruins. They don't want to reckon with the past. They so desperately want a blank slate that they'll burn the world beneath them to get it.

I have spent much of my adult life wondering "how much longer." When you and I first met, I spent the early days wondering how long it would be before you commented on how cold I was, how I never gave you indication of my feelings. I wondered when you'd realize that I don't feel like most people at all. I remember lying in your arms with your laptop on the table while a reporter streamed a wildfire. Live wires crackled, siding melted off of houses, flames danced in evil jubilee in all the windows, and a reporter told us through an N95 how a passing city had started it in the drought-dry brush, fans and engines stoking sparks which grew and raged. It could have been a power line, a pipeline, a server complex burning in the desert, a crypto mill burning coal. Just one of many sources, just the most visible excess, as the rich drift above us in their towering, electric arks.

Every time I'm out in the streets with chants in my ears and clashes with cops getting closer through the crowd, I think to myself this is when it will pop off. This is the time we will remember that the people who did this have names and addresses, and we will take the fight to them. We'll knock them out of the sky and their cities will come crashing down like meteors, and in the blaze they will be forced to reckon with the living. Every time I think, this is the last time we will do this.

But then I keep living. Many of us do.

#

We were out at your mother's farm for a birthday a few years ago, when we had the sense of what was coming but before what we know now. I remember it was a little gathering, a few people that you knew from your own childhood (funny how long the world's been like this) and I was in the kitchen with your mother. She was handing me food to bring out to the table, plastic gingham pinned down to the table with bag clips, blue-and-white china weighing down the corners. As she handed me deviled eggs, the last of the spread, she stopped me and said, "They talk about you a lot, you know."

Outside, your daughter was playing badminton with other children, a little close to the cattle fence but they were country kids, they knew what they were doing. In the sky above, a thick white contrail drifted through the blue, dissipating.

"Do they?" I asked, trying to hide my trepidation.

Your mother, I didn't have a read on her at the time. She was all short white hair and pleasant cheer, and a liberal insistence that I was waiting to result in a weird question at the wrong time. But you've trained her well, I think, and I have just been burned by generations of women I don't connect with, who mistake me for something I'm not.

She dried her hands on a canvas apron and said, "They think highly of your opinions."

I nodded, awkwardly.

"Are you planning to stay around?"

And she said it in such a way that I knew she didn't mean for dinner. Trapped, holding a plate of slippery deviled eggs, I realized I'd been cornered. Maybe she'd sensed my uncertainty. At the time, I had been planning to stay with you as long as it seemed right, but old women mean different things than I do. The kind of relationships they expect, dresses and suits and names on paper. Contractual things. Would I be so spooked if all my relationships weren't built on the ruins of things I rejected? It makes me think of my own lineage, of people who carved spaces for themselves in the gaps of others' lives. Children take spaces where adults don't fit, in the woods between the fields and the water towers. Adults who don't fit have to find their own trajectories, their own woods where others don't tread.

"I think so," I said, as honestly as I could.

Later, as you and your father were out feeding the animals, your mother and I were sitting on the porch with golden wine. People were leaving one by one, and the day was getting long and threadbare, like beloved yellow linen. The far-off thrum of fans and engines had started as the city made its circuit, and we could see the patches of blasted-dry land in the valley, the earth uninhabitable and scorched.

Then your daughter climbed up on the deck and sat at my feet, and it was the first time she seemed like she trusted me, rather than just that distant teacher-like respect. "Alyssa showed me the hayloft," she reported. "There are no adults allowed up there, though."

"Even if we're cool?" I asked, and she shook her head sadly, making your mother and me laugh.

"Sorry, no," she said, in the way kids mimic jokes they've heard. "You just don't make the cut."

The city appeared in the distance, rising up like a shining black moon over the tops of the hills, and your daughter watched it with a detached interest, something she'd seen often enough to no longer regard it with reverence. For me, though, it still felt recent – yet another new horror to reckon with. Another vast, damning excess.

And for a moment, we were three generations all stacked on top of each other, and time swept out before me like a landscape one could traverse, backwards and forwards, return to again and again. All things slotted beside one another in the fourth dimension, all people a piece of a continuous organism, all societies part of a continuous being for which we have no name, but which behaves according to a logic nonetheless. Progression, conflict, and transfiguration into a new form. At that moment, I was struck by the stasis and the motion of it, the repeating motifs and the new improvisations, the clash and churn of waves, by changing quantity deriving new quality. What is a long time, really, for a being like this? What is this new horror but just a different face of our same, old enemy?

I wondered then, as I wonder now, if we could go on like this, or if we would transform, or if we would end. As the city grew until it blotted out a piece of the sky, and the deafening roar filled the valley as it accelerated our end, I felt a great terror. Your mother shouted over it, pointing out the lights and signs on the silver-black buildings to your daughter, and I sat there feeling no awe, only cold fear. With the earth used, the rich flee again to the skies, to the stars, mocking us with their insulation from consequence.

The hot wind swept over us, and th" sun'sank and plunged us Into yellow and red and fading, waning blue.

#

At night, when our other partners and your daughter are asleep downstairs, I come up and sit with you as you work. The building where we live is leased, and our lives are still leased, and the heat gets hotter every day, but sometimes the fever breaks. I curl beside you as you read, and think of those who thought history was killed early in my life, and there was only one path into a shining, damned future. A whole lifetime ago, now.

The world has been like this for a long time. People have had so many convictions – that the world would end, that things would simply stop in perfect infinite globalized growth, that God would pass judgment and rain down fire. Now, staring down a fire artificial and godless, I wonder how long we will live like this, building in our own ruins until we run out of space to ruin. Living in the shadows of the cities overhead.

"Communists have to be optimists," you tell me, and I believe you. I do believe you, curled up like a fox beside you as the light burns slowly, and cicadas still rush outside the window, and night coils late but with still an infinity before dawn. You smell of sweetness and complication, and a love I'm glad you let me feel without demand or recourse. Something changing, and returning, and unforced.

"How will we know when we're beat?" I asked you once in a moment of despair.

And you remind me: "We have to be optimists. It's not up to us to say when we're through."

Don't make me go back to that empty house
Jessi Xiong

No!
Don't make me go back to that empty house
pack up nothing
leave the mess as evidence
signs of life, of love that once
took refuge here
now lost again, left behind
wandering.
The wind whistles through the windows
like the gaps between your teeth and
I find only traces of you, the loudest reminders of your absence.
Your hair is everywhere.
Soft, and already dead, like you.
You visited me in a half-dream
climbed into bed and laid on my chest
like you used to.
Eyes closed to the morning light
I raised both hands to touch you,
as real as you ever were.
Soft.
Against my wishes I floated to the surface of waking
your weight lifting off of me
the feeling of you slipping through my fingers again

I feel too light these days.
The day you left
someone scooped out my marrow,
hollow bird bones.
I hate coming home now
all the deserted spaces you used to fill scream at me
and I scream back
leave my broom untouched
let the dust settle into the abandoned spaces left in your wake,
because at least it's something,

more than nothing.
Dust, like you.
It's been almost three months and
I'm not moving on, but I guess I'm moving
and that is something,
more than nothing.
Although
some days I drag my feet
and other days I fall to my knees
and every now and then my heart cracks open again
like the first day I accepted you would be gone too soon
and I look up to stare straight through the atmosphere
searching for a dimension where we still exist
begging to a god I don't believe in,
Please!
Don't make me go back to that empty house.

Taxidermy
Sidney Rogers
after "What I Tell Myself Before I Sleep" by Jane Wong

When my mother — died I stored her body in a museum — I twisted her —
mouth until it made
the shape it used to make upon awakening — pensive and half-dream — I
hung her — fingers
from strings — fishing line and horse — hair tangling on their descent from
the ceiling — arms
outstretched she — the origami crane mid-flight — I painted her — glass
eyes in broken glass — eyeshadow — molded molten lead mascara on her —
lashes — called it a church window — I tied her — to a pane of plexiglass
— promised that it wouldn't shatter underneath her — feet — bare and
bony under grown — out nail polish — faded French tips— I wrote her —
notes on the back of a receipt — left it in her left — hand — labeled her as
"woman" and as — collection
number — (090265)— not as "mother" or — as "life lost" — I called it —
knowledge for the
future generations I — called it her body called — it her — legacy

Masoc(his)m

Rye Orrange

If words are an
Act of masochism then allow my life to be
Tied up and
tortured.

When my fingers find warmth where legs open and
tongues meet
We swallow vodka followed by pride
And home becomes
A euphemism for freedom.

I never feared public speaking, spiders
or dying young
But the unease that i've become the embodiment of my
Mother's worst fear
Threatened to terrorize my dreams most nights from age
Twenty-one through twenty-three and will perhaps trail me
Till thirty.

To grow into masculinity in your twenties is to sever a mother-
daughter relationship That was built on fraud and
Fallacy
And to uncover the best-kept secret that
To be a man is to never know the
Right words to say.

after memory
Hunter Dodrill

i keep seeing desire in other bodies   and calling it mine.   this longing so heavy

gravity called it god.   my chest an aching window   another word for grief

is toomuchlove.   profoundly human: the way your body fits in mine   home

-coming   -making   -going   a series of divine burdens i keep praying for.

A Haiku In Praise Of The Impact Of Estradiol And Spironolactone In Triggering A Second Puberty In Septuagenarians

Robin Elise Hamilton

Nine months in, my boobs
are now each quite a handful.
Hi, Joy! Hi, Rapture!

Appleseed
James Duque Huffman
ekphrastic poem based on Charles the First *by Jean-Michel Basquiat*

a sliver of silver
moonlight and
a golden bursting star
converse as
you hold
this red, red
apple in the
palm of your hand
take a bite, they say, take
a bite, they
want
to take a bite and you're
young and you're
so young, they say;
the tree from which you plucked
this fruit has
roots longer than your arm
could ever reach, but i'll reach you,
you say, i'll hold out this red
apple and you will bite until
your teeth crush the
seed and you will swallow one more
tiny poison
so you might speak another
tomorrow and
I will be here and
I will be young as this
fruit in my hand and one
day I will be old
as the orchard and I
will be old
as the soil itself if
you'll let me.

Acknowledgements

"The world has been this way for a long time." by Vincent Endwell first published by Radon Journal, January 2025